Tł
Cook Book

Fiona Munro

Illustrated by Nick Sharratt

FAMILY LEARNING

Kitchen Rules

Before you start, roll up your sleeves and put on an apron. Then wash your hands.

Get out everything you will need for a recipe before you start cooking.

Clean up as you work. Wipe up any spills right away.

When you have finished, remember to wash up.

Ask an adult to help when:

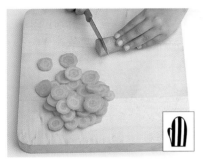

Cutting and slicing

Weighing and measuring

Using the oven

Watch for these symbols:

 Ask an adult to help.

 Turn on the oven with help from an adult.

Giant Rolls

You will need:

fork

sharp knife

table knife

tablespoon

mixing bowls

cutting board

butter

different kinds of rolls

To make egg and salami rolls, you will need:

2 hard-boiled eggs   sprouts   1 tablespoon mayonnaise

a pinch of salt

black pepper

salami

Try these fillings for the other rolls:

tomato   lettuce   cheese

ham   tuna

① Tap the eggs on the table, then peel the cracked shells. Wash off any bits of shell left on the eggs.

② In a clean bowl, mash the eggs with a fork. Mix in the sprouts, mayonnaise, salt, and black pepper.

③ On the cutting board, slice a roll in half with the sharp knife. Spread a little butter onto each half.

④ Spread a spoonful of the egg mixture evenly over the bottom half of the roll.

⑤ Take three slices of salami. Fold each in half, then in half again. Put this on top of the egg mixture.

⑥ Cover with the top half of the roll.

Your giant rolls could look like these:

Tuna roll

Ham and cheese roll

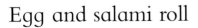

Egg and salami roll

Mini Pizzas

You will need:

cookie sheet

cutting board

teaspoon

bread knife

 350°F, 180°C

1 muffin for
each person

ketchup

mozzarella or
cheddar cheese

Choose from these toppings:

ham

mushrooms

olives

tuna

tomato

red pepper

pepperoni

① On the cutting board, slice the muffins in half with the bread knife.

② Spread a spoonful of ketchup onto each half.

③ Lay the cheese on top. Cover with your choice of toppings.

④ Put the mini pizzas on the cookie sheet.

⑤ Cook the mini pizzas for 10 minutes. When the cheese is melted and bubbling, they are ready.

Your mini pizzas could look like these:

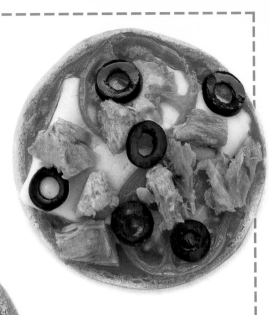

Tuna pizza

Cheese and ham pizza

Pepperoni pizza

Fruit Creams

You will need:

whisk

fork

tablespoon

mixing bowls

serving dishes

1¹⁄₂ cups strawberries

or 2 small bananas

1 cup heavy cream
(or yogurt)

2 tablespoons
sugar

Decorate your fruit creams using:

chocolate chips

cookies

seedless grapes

candied cherries

kiwi fruit

strawberries

① If you are using cream, whip it until it is thick.

② Use the fork to mash the strawberries or bananas until smooth. (Add a few drops of lemon juice to bananas to stop them from turning brown.)

③ Use the spoon to stir the cream or yogurt into the fruit. Add the sugar.

④ Spoon the mixture into serving dishes. Decorate your fruit creams.

Your fruit creams could look like these:

Bear cream

Creamy cat

Flower cream

Chocolate Chip Cookies

You will need:

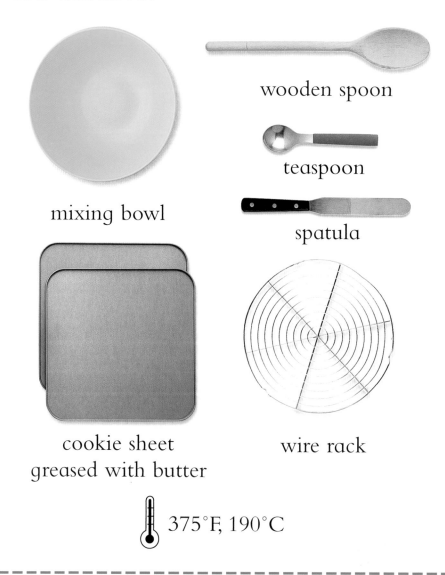

mixing bowl

wooden spoon

teaspoon

spatula

cookie sheet
greased with butter

wire rack

375°F, 190°C

To make 18 cookies, you will need:

8 tablespoons
soft butter

⅓ cup soft
brown sugar

⅓ cup sugar

 1 egg

½ teaspoon
vanilla extract

1 cup
all-purpose flour

½ teaspoon
baking soda

¼ teaspoon salt

1 cup
chocolate chips

① Put the butter and both sugars in the mixing bowl. Use the wooden spoon to beat until soft and creamy.

② Break the egg into the bowl. Beat the mixture until it is smooth.

③ Stir in the vanilla extract. Stir in the flour, salt, and baking soda, a little at a time.

④ Add the chocolate chips and stir until they are well mixed in.

5 Use the teaspoon to put small mounds of the mixture onto the cookie sheet. Leave plenty of space between each cookie.

6 Bake the cookies for 10 to 12 minutes, until they are golden brown.

7 Leave the cookies on the cookie sheet for 1 to 2 minutes to become firm. Then use the spatula to lift them onto the wire rack to cool.

Peppermint Patties

You will need:

2 mixing bowls

whisk

strainer

wooden spoon

cookie sheet lined with waxed paper

cutting board

fork

1 egg white

3 cups
powdered sugar

a few drops of
peppermint extract

a few drops of green
food coloring

a few drops of red
food coloring

Orange or lemon patties

Instead of using the peppermint extract and the red
and green food coloring, you can use:

a few drops of
orange juice

or a few drops of
lemon juice

a few drops of orange
food coloring

or a few drops of
yellow food coloring

1 In the large mixing bowl, whisk the egg white until it is light and frothy.

2 Sift the powdered sugar into the small bowl. Then stir the sugar into the egg white a little at a time

3 Using your hands, roll the mixture into a ball. Make a small dip in the middle and put in the peppermint extract. Knead the extract carefully into the ball.

4 Split the mixture int three balls. Knead red food coloring evenly into one ball and green food coloring evenly into another. Leave the last ball white.

5 For each color, roll the mixture into small balls and put them on the cookie sheet. Then flatten the balls with a fork and let them set overnight.

Why not invite your friends to a party?

Menu

Giant Rolls

Mini Pizzas

Fruit Creams

Chocolate Chip Cookies

Peppermint Patties